Race
Ahead
with
Reading

WANTED:
Prince Charming

By A. H. Benjamin

Illustrated by Fabiano Fiorin

W

For Izzy and Flynn – A.B.

Chapter One

Not very long ago lived a princess called Reverie. All she ever did was read fairytale books. And daydream of being rescued...

...by a knight in shining armour from the clutches of an evil dragon!

"Ahhhh," she would sigh. "Who will be my prince charming?" Princess Reverie was fed up with simply daydreaming. Why couldn't she be like a real fairytale princess? Sleeping Beauty, for instance.

"I'm beautiful," Princess Reverie said to herself. "All I need to do is sleep for a hundred years. Then surely my prince charming will come along..."

She tucked herself into bed.

Just then the chambermaid barged into the princess' bedroom. She plugged in the vacuum cleaner and started cleaning. Vroom! Vroom! Vroom!

VROOM

VROOM

Then the phone started to ring. Ring! Ring! Ring!

RIIING

Almost at the same time, the royal band began to play outside in the courtyard. Rompeta! Boom! Bang! Crash!

A large picture clattered to the floor. Crash!

7

"Argh!" screamed Princess Reverie, hands over her ears. "It's impossible to sleep for one minute let alone a hundred years!" She slipped out of bed and stomped out of the room.

Chapter Two

Later that day, Princess Reverie heard that a prince was holding a ball at his palace that very evening.

"I know!" she cried. "I'll be Cinderella!"

She at once began to get ready.

An hour before midnight, Princess Reverie arrived at the ball. She looked dazzling in her purple gown and glass slippers.

Everyone stopped what they were doing and stared at her… including the prince.

"Please allow me a dance," he invited.

"Of course," smiled Princess Reverie.

Oh, how they danced. They danced non-stop. Their feet hardly touched the floor as they twirled and swirled to the music.

Then the clock struck midnight.

"I must go now!" said Princess Reverie

all of a sudden. And she rushed off.

Of course, she made sure to leave behind

one of her glass slippers.

"Wait!" the prince called after her.

"You forgot something!"

And so saying, he kicked the glass slipper. It went sliding across the smooth floor and...

Crash!

It hit a wall, and broke into pieces.

"Oops!" giggled the prince, thinking it was funny. Princess Reverie was not amused.

"What kind of a prince are you?" she yelled, furious. "Certainly not charming!"
And she stormed off, hobbling a little.

Chapter Three

The next morning, Princess Reverie was reading the paper when when she saw an advert. It said: "Cleaner needed by seven dwarves living in a cottage in the heart of a wood. If interested apply to this number..."

"Perfect!" squealed Princess Reverie.

"I'll be Snow White!"

She applied for the job and got it.

The seven dwarves didn't turn out to be like Princess Reverie had imagined. They were dirty, lazy and rude. All they did was sit around, watching football on TV and playing computer games.

They stuffed themselves with pizzas and kebabs and guzzled fizzy drinks. They argued and fought and broke the furniture.

Princess Reverie got fed up with them all. "Why don't you go to work?" she shouted. "You know, in the mines like you're supposed to? To dig for diamonds?"

"No," they replied. "We've got everything we need here." It was all hopeless, thought Princess Reverie.

Even when someone knocked at the door it wasn't an ugly, old hag with a poisonous apple. It was just a delivery boy with more pizzas, kebabs and fizzy pop.

"No prince charming around here," she muttered and she left.

Chapter Four

A few days later, while brushing her hair,

Princess Reverie had an idea.

"How about Rapunzel?" she thought.

"Mmm, my hair is not long enough."

So she made herself a wig – the longest one in the world! She then hired a tall tower in the middle of the countryside.

Once there, she locked herself in and threw the key out of the top window. Before long she spotted a handsome young man driving past in a sports car.

"Here comes my prince charming!" smiled
Princess Reverie. She let her long wig drop
over the window sill until it touched the
ground below. Then, "Help! Help!" she
began to shout. "I'm stuck up here!
Please, help me!"

The young man saw and heard her.

He at once stopped the car.

"Hang on!" he shouted back.

He whipped out his mobile phone and

quickly dialled a number.

A few minutes later two fire engines arrived, sirens blaring and red lights flashing.

"Let go of me!" shrieked Princess Reverie as she was being rescued. "This is not what is supposed to happen! Let gooooo!"

But the firemen were having
no nonsense. Even when
Princess Reverie lashed
at them with her stupidly
long wig.

Chapter Five

One sunny day Princess Reverie was sitting in the palace gardens, daydreaming once more. "Ahhh," she sighed. "Who will be my prince charming?"

Suddenly, she heard Oink! Oink! Oink!

A large, purple pig with orange spots appeared out of nowhere.

"What a strange pig you are!" exclaimed Princess Reverie. "But you're so cute!"

And she planted a kiss on the pig's nose...

All of sudden – Piff! Paff! Puff!

And Princess Reverie turned into a purple pig with orange spots!

"At last!" cried the other pig. "I've been waiting years for this to happen!"

"What do you mean?" asked Princess Reverie, puzzled.

"I was once a prince," explained the other pig. "But a stupid witch turned me into a pig. Of course, she meant a frog. But she got the spell wrong!"

"I see," nodded Princess Reverie. "But aren't you supposed to turn into a prince again when a princess kisses you?"

"I wish!" replied the other pig. "That only happens when the witch gets the spell right."

"Great!" sighed Princess Reverie.

"Now what do we do?"

"We'll get married, of course!" replied the other pig. "Then we live happily ever after!"

"Oh, well," shrugged Princess Reverie.

"I don't see why not!"

"Lovely!" cried the other pig, delighted.

"By the way," he said as they trotted along together. "My name is... Prince Charming!"

First published in 2013 by
Franklin Watts
338 Euston Road
London
NW1 3BH

Franklin Watts Australia
Level 17/207 Kent Street
Sydney
NSW 2000

Text © A.H. Benjamin 2013
Illustration © Fabiano Fiorin 2013

The rights of A.H. Benjamin to be
identified as the author and Fabiano Fiorin
as the illustrator of this Work have been
asserted in accordance with the Copyright,
Designs and Patents Act, 1988.

Series Editor: Melanie Palmer
Editor: Jackie Hamley
Series Advisor: Catherine Glavina
Series Designer: Peter Scoulding

A CIP catalogue record for this book is
available from the British Library.

ISBN 978 1 4451 2645 6 (hbk)
ISBN 978 1 4451 2651 7 (pbk)
ISBN 978 1 4451 2663 0 (library ebook)

Printed in China

Franklin Watts is a division of Hachette
Children's Books, an Hachette UK company.
www.hachette.co.uk